# Oh, Sir Bragalot!

NEW FRONTIER PUBLISHING

*To Neve and Alex,*
*always—S D*

American edition published in 2022
by New Frontier Publishing Europe Ltd
www.newfrontierpublishing.us

First published in Great Britain in 2021
by New Frontier Publishing Europe Ltd,
Vicarage House, 58-60 Kensington Church Street, London W8 4DB
www.newfrontierpublishing.co.uk

Text and Illustrations copyright © 2021 Sharon Davey
The rights of Sharon Davey to be identified as the author
and the illustrator of this work have been asserted.
All rights reserved.

Distributed in the United States and Canada by Lerner Publishing Group Inc.
241 First Avenue North, Minneapolis, MN 55401 USA
www.lernerbooks.com

Library of Congress Cataloging-in-Publication data is available.

ISBN: 978-1-913639-97-6

Designed by Verity Clark · Printed in China

10 9 8 7 6 5 4 3 2 1

# OH, Sir Bragalot!

BY SHARON DAVEY

**M**eet **Sir Bragalot**, a **Knight** of the Round Table and an all-round, terrible **bragger** ...

He tells **unbelievable** tales!

"I'm great, I'm fantastic, don't you wish you were **ME**?!"

"I can jump **higher** than you!"

"Look at me! I can run **faster** than you!"

"I'm **stronger** than YOU!"

Oh, Sir Bragalot!

This went on for a LONG TIME. The other knights had heard all of his brags and boasts before—and they were bored, **bored**, **bored**!

One afternoon, when Sir Hector returned from a dangerous quest in a faraway land, King Arthur awarded him the Cross of Bravery.

Sir Bragalot didn't like
other knights getting medals
and trophies that *he* didn't have.

"I'm so much **BRAVER** than him!" boasted Sir Bragalot.

"I'm SO brave I could go on an even
**BIGGER** quest!" he bragged.

Suddenly, a squire came running in.

Sire, Sire, there's a dragon! Right outside the kingdom!

Who here will be our champion and defeat the dragon?

Sir Bragalot?

The knights were very happy to give Sir Bragalot this chance.

"Well, how about it, Sir Bragalot?"

"You are the **biggest**, **strongest**, and **bravest** of us all!"

"*I am?*" said Sir Bragalot. "I mean … er … **YES**, **I am**!"

Sir Bragalot set off on his noble quest with his knees knocking and his lips wobbling.

Sir Bragalot panicked. Bragging would *not* help him here.

# "M-m-mighty dragon, I'm here to slay you ... But, now that I am here,

I'm not very big or brave and, well ...

I'm sorry I lied about being the best.

I really don't want to be eaten.

Please?"

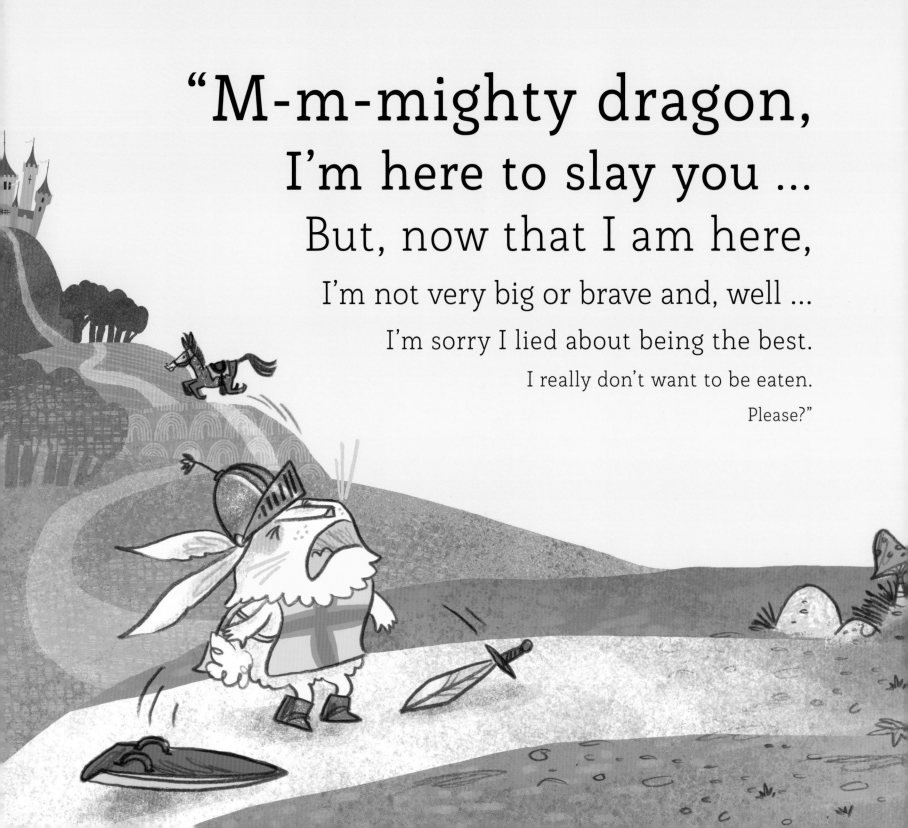

STOMP,

STOMP,

STOMP ...

Then out of the cave came ...

the teeniest, tiniest dragon you have ever seen.

"Why, you're so **SMALL**!"
Sir Bragalot squealed joyfully.

"You're tiny, you're teeny,
you're mini, you're weeny!"

Uh-oh. Here he goes again ...

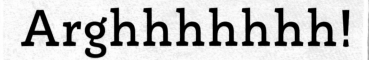

"I'm SOOOORRRYYY!"
cried Sir Bragalot!

And he never, ever bragged again ...

well, almost never.

"Did I ever tell you about the time I defeated a really **gigantic**, **super-enormous**, **dangerous** dragon? Once upon a time ..."